JOYRIDE

Dee Phillips

RiGHT NOW!

Blast
Dare
Dumped
Fight
Goal
Grind
Joyride
Scout

First published by Evans Brothers Limited
2A Portman Mansions, Chiltern Street, London W1U 6NR, United Kingdom
Copyright © Ruby Tuesday Books Limited 2009
This edition published under license from Evans Limited
All rights reserved

© 2011 by Saddleback Educational Publishing

ISBN-13: 978-1-61651-251-4
ISBN-10: 1-61651-251-2

Printed in Guangzhou, China
0112/CA21200022

16 15 14 13 12   2 3 4 5 6 7

Tanner, Hannah, Bailey and I.
The red car.
"Look," says Tanner. "The keys are inside!"

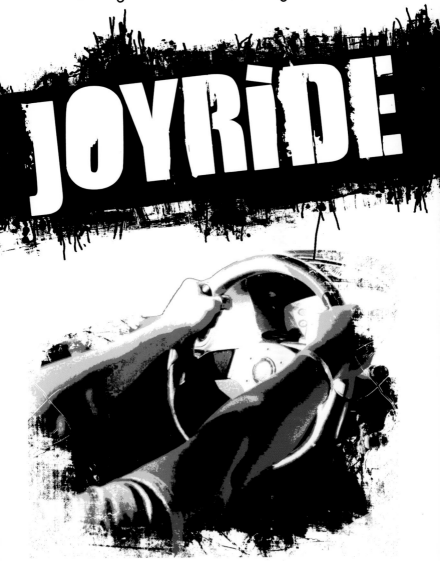

JOYRIDE

ONE MOMENT CAN CHANGE YOUR LIFE FOREVER

It's very cold.
It's very dark.
I can't move.
My legs hurt.
They hurt a lot.

I'm so scared that
I feel sick.

I can smell something.
Oh my God!
I can smell gas.
Why can I smell gas?
Why can't I move?

I'm so
scared...

...I'm going
to be sick!

I can see dark sky above me.
Dark sky and dark trees.
Where are we?
What happened?

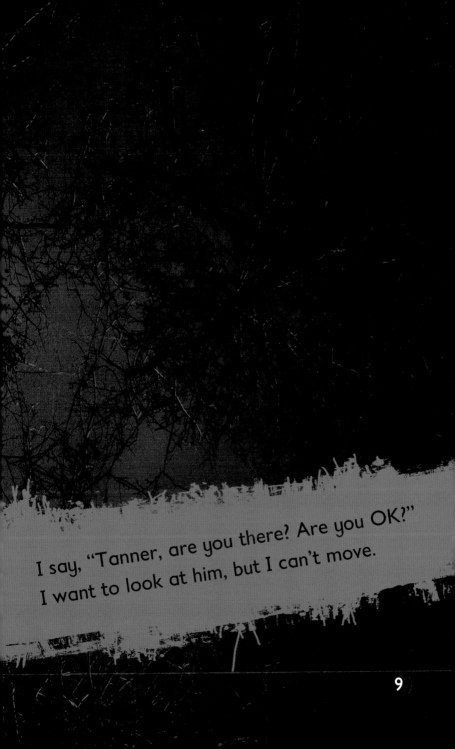

I say, "Tanner, are you there? Are you OK?"
I want to look at him, but I can't move.

I can hear Bailey crying.
I want to look at her, but I can't move.
I say, "It's OK, Bailey."
But she doesn't stop crying.

God. It's so cold.
So cold and dark.
I can't move.
I can't hear anything.
Just Bailey crying.

It's OK, Bailey, It's OK.

Hannah

Tanner

12

Jacob

Bailey

Bailey wasn't crying ten minutes ago.

She was laughing.

We were all laughing.

Tanner, Hannah, Bailey and I.

We were all messing around and laughing.

Then Tanner saw the car.
The red car.

Tanner loves cars.
Tanner has loved cars since
we were little kids.

"Look," said Tanner. "The keys are inside!"
He opened the driver's door of the car.

Tanner is crazy like that.
You never know what he will do next.

Tanner got into the driver's seat.
I opened the passenger door.
Tanner said, "Want to go for a drive, Jacob?"
That's just like Tanner!
He's been doing crazy stuff since
we were little kids.

19

Bailey and I got in the back of the car.
Hannah got in the front next to Tanner.
I put my arm around Bailey. It felt good.
Bailey was holding me tight.
She was laughing, but she was scared.

Tanner turned the key.
The car started.

We were all laughing.

The car started to move.

Ten miles an hour.

Thirty miles an hour.

Fifty miles an hour.

We were all laughing, but we were scared.

Tanner yelled, "I'm a good driver!"

Seventy miles an hour.

Ninety miles an hour.

Then Tanner hit a curb!

BANG!

Like a bomb.

0

140

160

180

200

Suddenly, the car was flying through the air.

Hannah was screaming.

Bailey was screaming, too.

FLYING

SCREAMING

The car flew through the air.
Then there was a noise like the
end of everything!

It's very cold.
I can't move.
My legs hurt a lot.
I'm so scared.

Now there are lights.

Flashing lights.

I want to cry.
I feel like a little kid.
A scared little kid.
I want to hold Bailey's
hand, but I can't move.
I say, "It's OK, Bailey.
The police are here."

A light shines in my face.
A man says, "It's OK, son. Hold on."
I like his voice. He sounds like my dad.

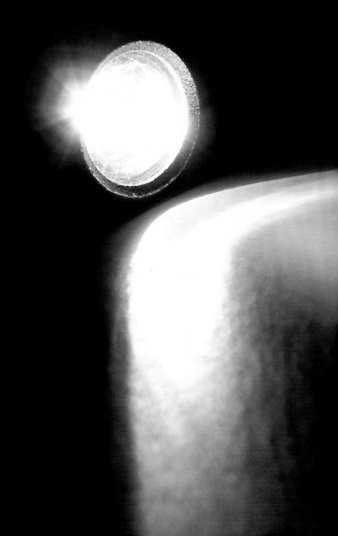

Another light shines into the car.
A woman says, "The girl is OK, too, sir."

We are in big trouble.

But the police sound OK.
I'm not so scared now.

I say, "Tanner. We are grounded forever!"
It makes me laugh.
Tanner and I grounded until we
are old men!

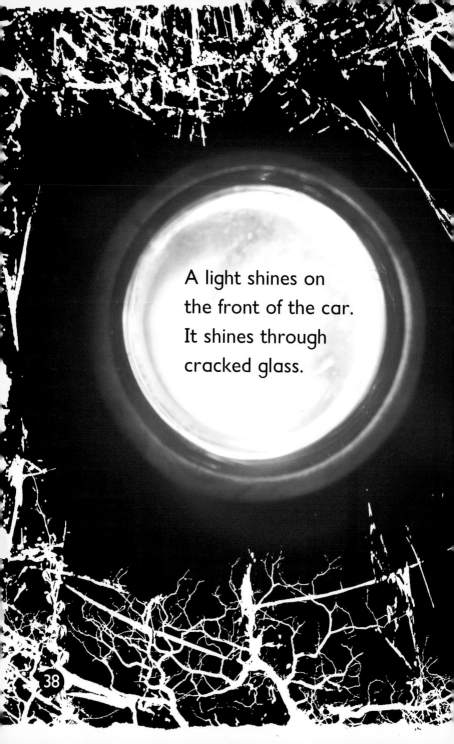

A light shines on
the front of the car.
It shines through
cracked glass.

The woman says, "What about the two in the front, sir?"

I hear the man's voice.
The man who sounds like my dad.

He says, "It's too late. There's nothing we can do for them."

It's very cold.

I can't move.

Everything hurts.

I'm going to be sick...

JOYRIDE—WHAT'S NEXT?

BEST FRIENDS
ON YOUR OWN

Makes everyone laugh

DANGER

Who is Tanner?

Hip-hop music

Cool
Funny
Lots of friends
Risky
Show-off
Thief

SPEED

Loves cars

Make a collage of words and pictures about Tanner or Jacob. Look for clues in the book and imagine:

- What things they like.
- What they like doing.
- What their friends think they are like.
- What they are really like.

WHAT IF?
WITH A PARTNER

Tanner and Jacob met when they were kids. Jacob knows Tanner is crazy, but he still gets into the car! Discuss:

- Why did Jacob get in?
- What might have happened if Jacob hadn't got in? What might Tanner have said?

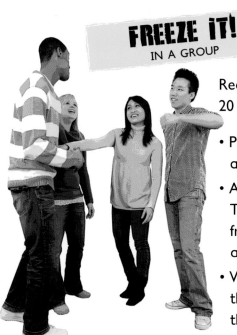

FREEZE IT!
IN A GROUP

Read and discuss pages 20 to 23.

- Plan a role-play and act it out for a friend.
- Act it out a second time. This time, ask your friend to shout "Freeze!" at some point.
- What is each character thinking and feeling at this point?

NEWS REPORT
ON YOUR OWN / WITH A PARTNER / IN A GROUP

Make a newspaper, radio, or TV report about the crash. Think about:

- The facts—where it took place, how fast the car was going, the type of car.
- What did Jacob and Bailey say about the crash?
- What did other people, such as the police or the friends' parents, say about the crash?

TEEN TRAGEDY

45

IF YOU ENJOYED
THIS BOOK,
TRY THESE OTHER
RiGHT NOW!
BOOKS.

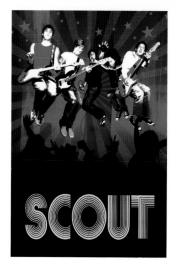

Tonight is the band's big chance. Tonight, a record company scout is at their gig!

Tonight, Kayla must make a choice. Stay in Philadelphia with her boyfriend Ryan. Or start a new life in California.

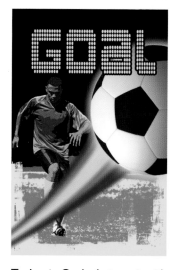

Today is Carlos's tryout with Chivas. There's just one place up for grabs. But today, everything is going wrong!

It's Saturday night.
Two angry guys. Two knives.
There's going to be a fight.

Taylor hates this new town.
She misses her friends.
There's nowhere to skate!

Damien's platoon is under
attack. Another soldier is in
danger. Damien must risk his
own life to save him.

It's just an old, empty house.
Kristi must spend the night
inside. Just Kristi and the
ghost...